memory of William F. Barber,
my ol' man

My Ol' Man

Patricia Polacco

Philomel Books

Whenever I get quiet and still inside and wish I was little again, all I have to do is think about my summers in Michigan. When I do this, it isn't now anymore, it is then again.

Our mom and dad were divorced and our summers were spent with our dad and grandma in the village of Williamston, just outside of Lansing.

There's our house on Middle Street. There's our grandma in the winderlight. She's watering her plants. Those are her crepe-paper parrots. There's Mr. Barkoviac, trying to get the mail past the Gaffners' dog.

There I am on the front porch with my brother, Richard.

"Do ya see him yet?" Ritchie asked as I leaned, almost tipping over the railing.

"Nope," I answered. "But he'll be here by four. Just like clockwork. He always is."

We were referring to our ol' man.

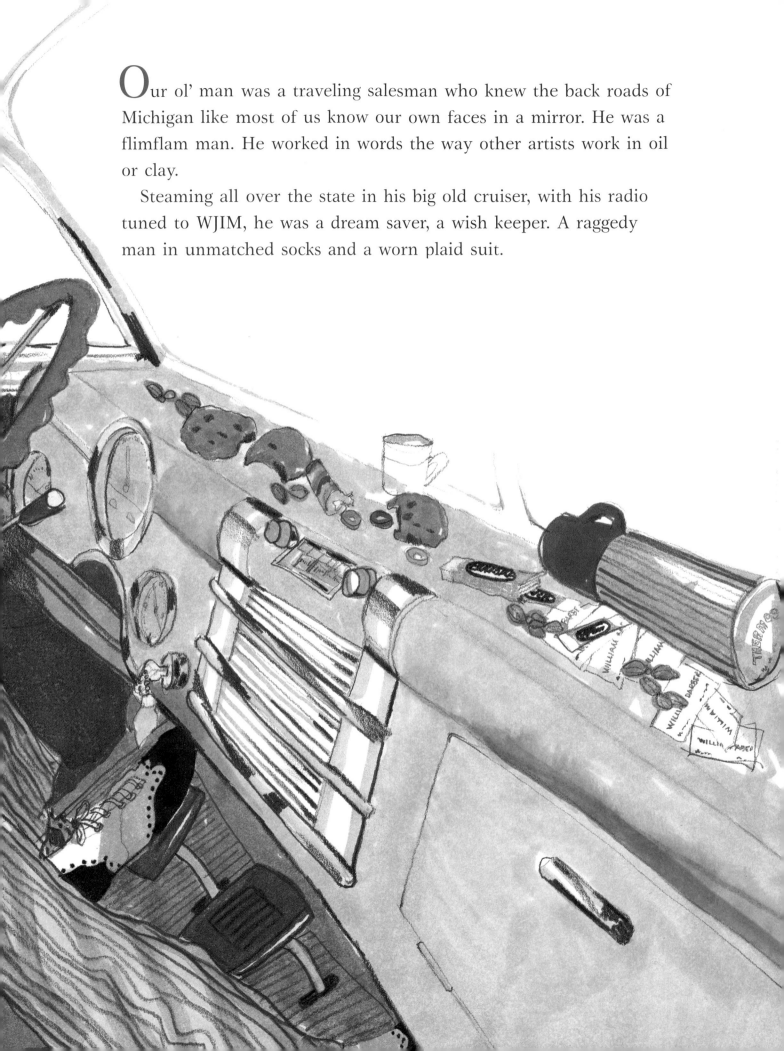

Our ol' man was a traveling salesman who knew the back roads of Michigan like most of us know our own faces in a mirror. He was a flimflam man. He worked in words the way other artists work in oil or clay.

Steaming all over the state in his big old cruiser, with his radio tuned to WJIM, he was a dream saver, a wish keeper. A raggedy man in unmatched socks and a worn plaid suit.

Every single day of his life on the road, he brought home a tale to tell us. He collected stories like kids collect baseball cards, or fine ladies collect special teacups.

When he'd pull up, he'd always spin us a good yarn. Like how Eldie Dunkle got his heel caught in the train tracks when the 4:33 was barreling down at him out of Fowlerville. Or how he personally saw the Bender sisters buy chewing tobacco over at Fates Pharmacy. "Fer the hired hand," they'd say, but everybody knew it was for them.

But he never had a story that changed so many things for Ritchie and me as the day he glided home in his big ol' cruiser, stepped out, and said, "You'll never guess what happened today in that-there machine."

His eyes were blazing. We knew this was going to be the mother of all stories.

We slid to our knees to hear better.

"I was making my way out near Rowley Church. Driving along, sweet and easy, when near Aunt Elisa's woods the machine stopped, all by itself. I just sat there."

"What happened then, Da?" we asked in a whisper.

"I got out of the car and walked straight into the woods and found myself smack next to Potter's Pond."

"What happened then, William?" Gramma asked as she wheeled into the room.

"Well, sir, that's when I saw it!"

"Saw what?" we asked.

"You'll have to see it for yourself to believe it!" he said as he squinted his eyes, serious-like.

We steamed out on Dietz Road to the exact spot where the car stopped for Dad. It stopped again, gentle-like, without a sound. We followed Dad into the woods until he brought us to Potter's Pond. Then he stopped and pointed.

It was a rock. A great huge rock.

My brother howled in disbelief. "Aw, Da, it's just an old rock."

"Give a chance, Ritchie boy. Keep looking," my dad coaxed. "I thought it was just a rock too until. . . . There's magic in that rock."

I kept looking and looking until I couldn't look away.

"It's just a dumb ol' rock," Ritchie kept saying.

"C'mon, Ritchie, look at it!" I said. You see, I knew my brother needed magic more than any of us. He hadn't been the same since my mom and dad got their divorce. I walked over and started touching that rock. "Why, there's lines in it. They look really old too!"

Now, without saying a word, Ritchie went up and touched the lines in the rock. One by one. "It *is* magic," he whispered.

We burst into the parlor, telling Gramma about the magic rock. It didn't matter to any of us what the magic was yet. We knew it was there, all right.

"Ma," Dad said, "what I can't figure out is that I grew up just over the holler from that pond. I swam there almost every day in the summer. I don't recall ever seeing that rock before."

"That certainly is strange, isn't it," Gramma said thoughtfully.

"It's so old," Ritchie whispered.

"Like it's been there forever," I agreed.

Ritchie started singing and dancing around the room. "Here comes the magic," he kept singing. "Here comes the magic."

"I haven't seen that boy smile like this for ever so long," Gramma said. "That's magic enough for me."

I just wondered how the magic was going to happen to us.

A few days later, nearabout noon, Ritchie and I were making crepe-paper parrots with Gramma—she made the parrots to remind her of Florida, a place she wanted to go someday. She painted glorious oil paintings too, even though her hands were crippled with arthritis. In fact, this was the summer that she was going to teach me to use oil paint . . . on real canvas. But we were cutting out crepe paper when the front door opened.

It was our ol' man!

"William, what are you doing home so early?" Gramma asked.

"Sales are down. Times are hard. Varney had to let me go today," Da said as he tried to smile.

I couldn't believe it. My dad, fired!

"We'll get by, William," my gramma said softly as she touched his hand.

Now, Gramma and my ol' man lived from day to day even in the best of times. About all the money he ever had at one time rattled in his front pocket. "We may be boot-poor, but we're rich on dreams," he used to say.

Ritchie and I knew that his news wasn't good.

The next morning Ritchie and I overheard Da tell Gramma he'd have to sell his car. "I can't keep up with the payments," he said. I thought of that old cruiser, and how the sunlight caught the chrome on the bumper, and how Da's stories all seemed to come from that car.

"You can't, Da," Ritchie burst out.

"Son, I'm going to have to put an ad in the *Enterprise* today," Dad said softly.

"No, Da . . . let's go to the rock," Ritchie pleaded. "If it's really magic, it'll help."

Dad agreed, but when we got out there it just seemed like a big old rock. Ritchie put his hands on it. "I don't feel anything anymore," he said through bitter tears.

Then we all put our hands on the rock. The three of us together traced our fingers right across the old mysterious lines.

Our ol' man felt it first. "I feel something!" he said, his eyes glowing.

I waited, and there it was. "I do too!" I said. "I feel like laughing, only it's inside."

"I feel like I could just lift right off the ground!" Ritchie said breathlessly.

"By golly, you're right," Dad said, and he jumped up on the rock. "The magic is here!"

Now, we still didn't know exactly what the magic was, but we knew things were going to get better.

Another week went by. Then one day as I was looking at the paint set in the window at Baldino's, I heard Mrs. Baldino say, "Lookin' at them paints again?"

As I started to leave, she took the paint set out of the window and handed them to me. "They're yours. Canvases too. Your gramma paid for 'em, said to give 'em to you when you came by."

I knew where the rock's magic had gone. Then I looked up and saw Gramma's beautiful parrots hanging in the middle of the store. For sale.

When I saw the empty winderlight that afternoon, I started to cry. "Gramma, your parrots were the next-best thing to goin' to Parrot Jungle in Florida."

"Oh, child," she said as she hugged me, "you need those paints just now more than I need to see Parrot Jungle. And a promise is a promise: I said I'd teach you to paint, and I will."

Each day my dad went out and did odd jobs to keep food on the table, and each day Gramma and I worked hard on a painting that was to be a surprise for my ol' man.

Da's cruiser didn't sell and didn't sell, and one day the finance company called to say they were going to take Da's car back. I was beginning to wonder about the magic. Why wasn't it working? But our ol' man believed. Almost every day he'd steam out to Potter's Pond and sit by that old rock with Ritchie and me.

But after a time Ritchie wouldn't go anymore.

Then one day there was a knock on the front door.

"Guess they're picking up the car today," Gramma said sadly.

I went to get Dad. The man shoved a piece of typed paper into my dad's chest. "Are you the man who wrote this and sent it in to the radio station?"

"Yessir, that's my story, all right," our dad answered.

"Well, Bill Barber, I want to shake your hand! That-there is some amazing rock you wrote about!"

"Rock?" Ritchie and I said.

"Son, I'm not here about that rock. I'm here because of magic, hope, and dreams! These days we've got precious little of that! Anyone who can write those words when he's down-and-out is the kind of man other people need to listen to!"

Dad looked puzzled.

"Mister, I'm offering you a job . . . on the radio! We need people like you at WJIM!"

Dad had written about that old rock and the strange and mysterious lines on it and how we felt its magic. My heart sang just to think about him rollin' all over the Midwest in that old cruiser with the sunlight gleaming on his bumper. He'd be collecting stories, just like always, only instead of just tellin' us, he'd be tellin' them to everybody. On WJIM!

"And sometimes you three can come with me," he said. "Maybe someday we'll go all the way down to Florida. All the way to Parrot Jungle!"

Well sir, I'm about to tell you, the most mysterious thing about that old rock happened next. We all steamed out to Aunt Eliza's woods that very day. We waded the creek to Potter's Pond. We wanted to say thank you in some way to that old rock.

But when we got there, the rock was gone. Not a trace of it.

"But it was right here, right here!" my brother yelled as he pointed to the spot where it had been.

"No sign of it," Dad said almost in a whisper.

Just then the sun streamed through the trees above and made a shaft of light that beamed right where the rock had been.

"But, Da, what will we do for magic now?" I asked. Then the light got brighter. I think that it was at that exact moment that I knew the magic was inside of us. It had been there all along.

All the way back home, Ritchie complained he'd never see the rock again, but I had a surprise of my own. When we got back, I unveiled the painting I had been working on. It was of Potter's Pond and the wonderful rock!

"There it is, Ritchie, old lines and all."

The look of wonder that appeared on my brother's face never left his eyes again.

The magic of that summer lives in my heart to this day. The rock was magic, all right, but the real magic was the memory of my ol' man. Anytime I want, I get quiet and still inside, and I am little again. I think of that summer by Potter's Pond.

I have the gift of that memory anytime I recall it. A memory that brings back Gramma, the parrots, the cruising machine, and, most especially, my ol' man. A memory that will last as long as children tell others about fathers they love.

Me at age 7

Da by the winderlight, holding Steven

Da, Gramma and me with my
Traci and Steven

Philomel Books, a division of The Putnam & Grosset Group,
200 Madison Avenue, New York, NY 10016. Published simultaneously in Canada. Printed in Singapore.
Book design by Donna Mark. Hand-lettering by David Gatti. The text is set in Gamma Book. Philomel Books,
Reg. U.S. Pat. & Tm. Off. Library of Congress Cataloging-in-Publication Data. Polacco, Patricia. My Ol' Man /
Patricia Polacco. p. cm. Summary: A girl recalls the special summer spent in Michigan with her yarn-
spinning father and a magic rock. [1. Fathers—Fiction. 2. Magic—Fiction. 3. Rocks—Fiction. 4. Storytelling—Fiction.]
I. Title. II. Title: My Old Man. PZ7.P75186Mx 1995 [E]—dc20 94-15395 CIP AC ISBN 0-399-22822-5
5 7 9 10 8 6 4